For daughter Elisse, son Waylen and grandson Ellery—SM, RM

For the Ando family—and for the Spencers, a family that loves animals.
Also a big thank you to Slavia, Roy and Elisse; and to Carol, Michael and
Elisa for enabling me to illustrate this remarkable story—MA

LIBRARY AND ARCHIVES CANADA CATALOGUING IN PUBLICATION

Title: Peggy's impossible tale / Slavia & Roy Miki ; illustrations by Mariko Ando.
Names: Miki, Slavia, author. | Miki, Roy, author. | Ando, Mariko, illustrator.
Identifiers: Canadiana 2021013240X | ISBN 9781926890210 (hardcover)
Classification: LCC PS8626.I419 P44 2021 | DDC jC813/.6—dc23

Art direction by Carol Frank · Book design by Elisa Gutiérrez
The text of this book is set in Winslow. Chapter titles are set in Barteldes.

10 9 8 7 6 5 4 3 2 1
Printed and bound in Canada on ancient-forest-friendly paper.

The publisher thanks the Government of Canada, the Canada Council for the Arts and
Livres Canada Books for their financial support. We also thank the Government of the
Province of British Columbia for the financial support we have received through the
Book Publishing Tax Credit program and the British Columbia Arts Council.

Slavia Miki & Roy Miki

Peggy's Impossible Tale

Illustrations by

Mariko Ando

TRADEWIND BOOKS
Vancouver · London

Contents

I am Peggy and I am a guinea pig. This is my true story.

CHAPTER ONE

Home Free

I was alone in my cage at Noah's Ark Pet Store. The door opened and the bell chimed.

A woman and a young girl came in the store. "Hi, Sandy, I'm Christine. We talked on the phone yesterday."

"Yes, I remember. You're looking for a pet."

"Can you help my daughter, Lisa, choose one?"

"Absolutely," Sandy answered. "How about a guinea pig? They're easy to care for, and they love to sit on your lap and be petted." She laughed. "Probably because they're too stupid to do anything else."

"Hey, Sandy, I'm not stupid," I squeaked right back. "I can understand you."

Lisa stopped at Simon's cage. He was a tortoiseshell with dark eyes and patches of

red and black fur. Lisa spent a long time with Simon. I hoped she wouldn't choose him.

Then Lisa spotted Emily. She was a Peruvian with long sweeping silver hair covering her eyes. To me she looked like a well-groomed dust mop. Lisa seemed drawn to Emily. I hoped, I hoped she wouldn't choose her.

I'm just an ordinary guinea pig with short white hair and small pink ears. I was afraid that Lisa wouldn't choose me.

I raced back and forth in my cage, squeaking as loud as I could, "Look at me! Look at me!"

"Isn't she the cutest!" Lisa exclaimed.

She noticed me!

"Would you like to hold her?" Sandy asked.

When the cage door opened, I jumped into Lisa's arms.

Lisa smothered me in kisses. I kissed her back. I knew right then that Lisa and I would be best friends.

"You need a name," Lisa said. "How about Peggy? Do you like Peggy?"

I did like the name Peggy. And I liked Lisa too.

Home I went with Lisa.

Finally I had a family of my own.

CHAPTER TWO

Under Cover

That first night, Lisa hid me under her bedcovers. They were feather-fluffy and light as air.

"When you raced around and squeaked to get my attention, I knew you were smart. And when you kissed me, I knew immediately that we would become best friends."

Lisa believed in me!

"We *will* be best friends," I squeaked loudly.

Lisa hushed me. "Shhhh, I don't want my mom and dad to see you when they come in to say goodnight."

I washed my paws and face, scrubbed behind my ears, then curled up under Lisa's bedcovers and fell asleep.

CHAPTER THREE

Checking In

My first few weeks whizzed by as I learned many new things. I loved my new home. There was a bedroom with a woodchip bed and an exercise room with monster-sized mirrors that reflected me and me and me. There was a balance ball—over and over, it rolled me over. It was impossible to stay atop. There was a hop-on, hop-off wheel that ran me round and around. What a dizzying ride.

CHAPTER FOUR

Busy Buddies

Lisa spent all her spare time with me. "I wish we could talk to each other," she said.

That's when I set out to teach her my squeak talk. For five days I repeated my squeaks until Lisa finally understood me.

Sometimes Lisa talked and I listened.

Sometimes I talked and Lisa listened.

Sometimes we sat in silence.
Just like best friends do.

Sometimes we danced, twirling and swaying to the beat of our favourite music.

Sometimes we had picnic lunches of lettuce-leaf sandwiches, plums and pears—all set out on a baby-blue blanket.

Through it all, we talked and talked and talked.

And sometimes we danced some more.

CHAPTER FIVE

Time Telling

I told time by the rhythm of each day. Sunrise was time for me to wake up and eat my breakfast. At noon, the cuckoo cuckoo clock told me it was time for lunch. Five o'clock was dinner time—time for family conversations and delicious morsels from the table. Evening was relaxing time—time for watching TV and playing games. When night came, I dreaded it—bedtime.

The best time of day was three-thirty in the afternoon. I could hardly wait. That's when Lisa came home from school. Even before she stepped on the front stairs, I would squeak, "Welcome home, welcome home."

"You're so smart, Peggy," Lisa said one day. "You can tell time."

CHAPTER SIX

Step by Step

"Want to study upstairs?"
I wanted to go with Lisa, but I couldn't. The stairs rose like a mountain. I tried and tried, but I kept tumbling down. Climbing stairs was impossible.

Seeing me struggle, Lisa's mom gave me her best advice ever. "The difficult is done immediately. The impossible takes a little longer."

"We'll try again tomorrow," Lisa said.

Yes, tomorrow, I will try again tomorrow.

Day after day we tried. No luck. Until, one day, Lisa put my paws on a step and gave my round bottom a little push. To my surprise I climbed one stair, and then another, one by one, all the way to the top, all by myself.

I could finally climb stairs.

CHAPTER SEVEN

Litter Bit

It was wintertime in Vancouver.

"You can tell by the steady rain," Lisa said.

Michael, Lisa's dad, chimed in, "Don't worry. The sun will come out again soon."

Since we couldn't go outside, Lisa thought it would be fun for me to run around the house. "It will expand your world," she said.

The whole house to play in—what a great idea. I was ready to leave my shelter for new adventures and places unknown.

Lisa asked, "Mom, can Peggy run around the house?"

"On one condition," Lisa's mom replied. "Peggy has to use a litter box."

What's a litter box?

The next day Lisa set a small box on the floor, pointed to it and said, "That's a litter box. Use it and you can run around the house."

"Use it? For what?"

"To pee, silly."

CHAPTER EIGHT

Room Roaming

We lived in a three-storey house. I intended to check out every floor and every room. My adventure began.

I found doors shut tight, doors left ajar, doors that led to hallways, and hallways that led to rooms with mysterious dark closets. Racks of clothes, abandoned and forgotten, hung like ghosts on bent wire hangers.

Did ghosts wear suits?

CHAPTER NINE

Attic Escapade

It was in the spider-webbed silence of the attic that I discovered hot-air vents. I loved how they blew warm air in my face and made my hair stand up in spikes.

What's in there? I poked my head, shoulders and tummy through the open vent. To my horror I saw nothing but a dark and bottomless hole. I twisted and turned. Stuck! How will anyone find me? I cried my squeaky cries until I was exhausted.

Suddenly I heard footsteps. "Peggy! Peggy! Where are you?"

It was Lisa.

Hot-air vents are dangerous. Wisely, I never went near them again.

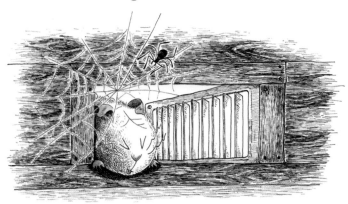

CHAPTER TEN

Hot-Wired

It was in the study of Lisa's dad that I discovered electrical plugs—in a shocking way.

Lisa warned me not to touch them. "They'll curl your hair," she said, laughing.

Still, I couldn't resist. Zap! Ouch! I pulled back my paw. Lisa was right. I liked my hair exactly as it was, so I stayed away from the plugs—far away.

Cords galore everywhere on the floor. I shuffled them about, enjoying the sound of their clatter. They were just the right size, just right for chewing. But zap! Ouch! Shocked again. My teeth rattled and my body shook.

Wires, they too are best avoided.

CHAPTER ELEVEN

Surround Sound

Different sounds filled the house.

The ding-donging doorbell signalled a visitor.

Who was outside? Time to be cautious. Lisa peeped through the peephole.

With lightning speed, the beeping microwave cooked fast food fast. Something yummy was on its way.

The talking picture box was the family's favourite. It became mine too. Lisa's dad made popcorn, and we all snuggled together on the caramel-coloured couch. It was movie-watching time. Sometimes laughing, sometimes crying, we shared bowls of buttered popcorn and sipped sodas through straws.

One sound terrified me—the deep grumbling of the monster air-sucking machine. Back and forth, back and forth, it moved along the floor. With its huge round belly and slinky long nose, it sucked up everything in its path, never to be seen again. Would I too be sucked up, never to be seen again? Time to hide behind the couch. Vacuum was coming!

CHAPTER TWELVE

Lights Out

When bedtime came, I never wanted to go to sleep. I found that I could stay up longer if I played a game of CHASE with the family.

I was fast and hard to catch. I sped around corners, racing from one room to the next, under chairs and tables, and darting over pillows on the floor. I hid behind the curtains. Hearing footsteps, I ran to my perfect hiding place among the pots and pans.

"Peggy, Peggy, where are you?" Lisa called.

Lisa's dad too called, "Peggy, Peggy, where are you?"

I was silent as a mouse. If they couldn't find me, they couldn't catch me.

The game would go on and on for over an hour. It ended only when Lisa dropped a blanket over me like a parachute. I was captured! We all laughed and laughed. Only then would I concede defeat and go happily to bed.

CHAPTER THIRTEEN

Buckle Down

It was no longer winter. The rains had stopped and there were promises of sunny days.

"Let's go for a walk," Lisa said. "I made a little harness for you."

I was excited to take my first trip outdoors in my new harness, but walking with it was impossible.

I tried seventeen times, but over and over, I tipped over. Lisa's mom reassured me, "The difficult is done immediately. The impossible takes a little longer."

Finally I learned the art of leash walking.

CHAPTER FOURTEEN

Tripping Out

One Saturday morning, Lisa and I went for a walk. I liked how the cool grass tickled my toes. But when I rubbed my face in it, I sneezed. "Achoo, achoo."

I wondered if grass tasted as good as it smelled. It sure did.

But just as I was enjoying myself, I learned a word for danger: Cat.

"That's a Siamese," Lisa explained.

"Hello," I squeaked.

I thought we could be friends, but Cat was not at all friendly. She spit, hissed and arched her back. Her hair stood up like a porcupine's. That made her look so funny I squeaked at the sight of her. I guess she didn't like my sense of humour, because she swatted my head with her paw. Why didn't Cat like me?

I needed to be careful whenever I was near Cat. So I was.

Soon I learned another word for danger: Crow. I often saw Crow watching us as he perched in the tall maple tree in front of our house. Sometimes he followed us down the sidewalk, flying from tree to tree. One day he swooped down on me. I felt the whooshing of his wings, then a peck on my head. Ouch! Crow, with sharp beak, I needed to watch out for him. So I did.

CHAPTER FIFTEEN

Friendly Fanny

On Wednesdays, Lisa and I went for our regular walks. One afternoon a little dog came running, barking all the way. I squeaked in fright. Lisa waved and called, "Hi, Betty. Hi, Fanny."

"Betty and Fanny are our neighbours," Lisa said. "They live two doors down from us."

When Betty saw me, she shrieked, then laughed hysterically.

What's so funny?

"Betty thinks you're a rat."

How could she mistake me for a rat? I'm no rat.

"I'm sorry for mistaking you for a rat," Betty said. "I want you to meet my dog, Fanny. She's a poodle."

Seeing them together made me squeak with laughter. I couldn't stop. It wasn't polite to laugh, but Betty and Fanny looked like identical twins with their short, curly copper-coloured hair.

Fanny barked and wagged her tail hello. I liked her. We became friends, unlike Cat or Crow.

After that, Lisa and I often walked with Betty and Fanny. On one walk, Crow swooped down on me again. In an instant, Fanny pounced. Crow flew off. Even Cat kept her distance when Fanny was with me. Fanny was my own superhero.

CHAPTER SIXTEEN

That's Impossible

"Lisa, I'm so impressed with all the things Peggy has learned to do," Lisa's mom said. "I'm going to phone Sandy at the pet store. She'll be so surprised."

"Hi, Sandy, this is Christine. Do you remember the guinea pig you suggested as a pet for my daughter, Lisa? Well Peggy is very smart. She has even learned to climb stairs and walk on a leash."

When Lisa's mom hung up the phone, she said to Lisa, "Sandy says it is absolutely impossible for Peggy to climb stairs and walk on a leash. She'd have to see it to believe it. She says if we think Peggy is so special, we should enter her in the Special Pets Contest that's being held next weekend."

"Let's do it," Lisa replied.

"Yes! Let's just do it," I squeaked.

CHAPTER SEVENTEEN

Show Time

Lisa's dad drove us to the Special Pets Contest.

We saw many beautiful and remarkable pets. They certainly looked special. How could I ever compete with them?

There was a golden labradoodle whose coat was shaved short except for tufts of hair on his tail and long legs. His head looked like the mane of a lion. He was proud and regal as he strutted by. I didn't look regal with my short legs, and I didn't have an impressive lion's mane—or any tufts of hair either.

There was a cockatoo with long beautiful bright feathers. How could my short white coat ever compete with her?

There was a long slithery snake with scary shiny scales. It hissed, raised its head menacingly high, then coiled itself back into a ball. I wished I had scary shiny scales like Snake.

More special pets arrived—a blue iguana, a peacock spider and a large mata mata turtle. I hoped I wouldn't disappoint Lisa.

Pet after pet came into the judges' circle.

That's when I saw Cat. Oh she was beautiful all right, but she still did not want to be friends. She gave me a stern look of warning, hissed and swiped at me as she slinked by.

Cat stepped into the judges' circle. She performed perfect yoga poses with grace. The judges were impressed.

When our turn came, the judges asked Lisa, "Why do you think your pet is special?"

Lisa answered, "Peggy climbs stairs and walks on a leash."

"Absolutely impossible!" the judges said in unison. I was surprised to see that Sandy was one of the judges.

With leash in hand, Lisa and I walked to the stairs. I climbed them easily—up and down. The judges shook their heads in disbelief.

"I had to see it to believe it!" Sandy exclaimed.

It seemed impossible—but I won the contest.

CHAPTER EIGHTEEN

Wisdom Wise

It was past my bedtime when Lisa and I arrived home. We were too excited to sleep. We talked late into the night about the day's events, especially about winning. All my fears and difficulties were forgotten.

Lisa was proud of me. "You are so special. You won the contest because you did things the judges believed were impossible for a guinea pig to do."

I kissed Lisa's cheek.

"You're special too!" I squeaked. "You believed in me, and the impossible became possible, even for an ordinary guinea pig like me."

"The difficult is done immediately," Lisa's mom reminded us as she passed by. "The impossible takes a little longer."

She's so right!

Lisa and I giggled together under her bedcovers. They were feather-fluffy and light as air.

Acknowledgements

Peggy is based upon actual events in the lives of our daughter, Elisse, and her guinea pig, Peggy. Elisse's love for Peggy transformed her from an ordinary guinea pig into an exceptionally special one. Overcoming her initial fears and limitations, Peggy accepted any challenge, just so they could be together, at least so it seemed to us. Peggy was intelligent and loving with a great sense of humour. Her "joke" of suddenly popping high up into the air like a Mexican jumping bean scared the heck out of us. Of course, it initiated her favourite game of CHASE with the family. The relationship between Elisse and Peggy enriched our lives, showing us how Elisse's love could transform and elevate the life of even the smallest of beings. Peggy's love for Elisse showed us how the seemingly impossible could become possible and how the ordinary could become special.

After completing her kinesiology degree, Elisse went on to become a Registered Massage Therapist. She recalled her childhood love of horses, years of riding lessons and how she dreamed of one day working with both humans and horses. At the time it seemed an impossible dream. It was during a trail-riding excursion that she met Sparky, a seriously injured horse. Knowing his certain fate, she purchased Sparky and successfully rehabilitated him using her knowledge as a kinesiologist, exercise physiologist and RMT. This decision to rehabilitate Sparky was fateful, leading as it did to years of intense studies in equine therapy, and later becoming a certified Equine Assisted Learning Instructor. Elisse went on to rescue three other horses, Waco, Mystey and Thunder, rehabilitating their physical and emotional traumas. Just as her loving relationship with Peggy had elevated Peggy's natural abilities, so too her loving relationship with her four horses elevated their natural abilities so that they could become therapy horses.

In a moment of epiphany Elisse's career was brought full circle: her two passions, human therapy and equine therapy, became one when she partnered her four special therapy horses with her human clients in specifically designed programs through Equilibria Therapeutics, a business she created and operates. Her seemingly impossible dream became a reality.

"The difficult is done immediately. The impossible takes a little longer."

..

We want to thank Michael Katz for his superb advice and patient guidance throughout the writing process, and thanks to Carol Frank for so enthusiastically supporting our Peggy project and for her brilliant work as art director of this book. Kudos to Elisa Gutiérrez for her exceptional work as book designer. Thanks also to Carol for connecting us with Mariko Ando. Mariko's artwork is stellar in revealing the unfolding of Peggy's impossible tale.